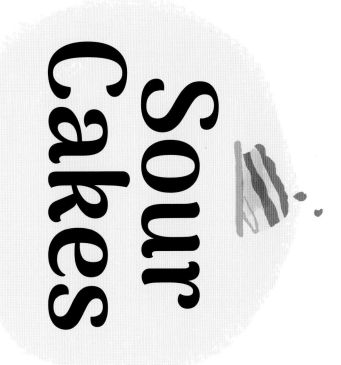

For my sour cakes, with love—K.K.

For my mom and siblings, for putting up with me at my most sour—A.K.

Text © 2021 Karen Krossing | Illustrations © 2021 Anna Kwan

Owlkids Books acknowledges the financial support of the Canada Council for the Arts, the Ontario Arts Council, the Government of Canada through the Canada Book Fund (CBF) and the Government of Ontario through the Ontario Creates Book Initiative for our publishing activities.

Published in Canada by Owlkids Books Inc., 1 Eglinton Avenue East, Toronto, ON M4P 3A1

Published in the US by Owlkids Books Inc., 1700 Fourth Street, Berkeley, CA 94710

Library of Congress Control Number: 2020951497

Library and Archives Canada Cataloguing in Publication

Title: Sour cakes / written by Karen Krossing ; illustrated by Anna Kwan.
Names: Krossing, Karen, author. | Kwan, Anna, 1991- illustrator.
Identifiers: Canadiana 20200409948 | ISBN 9781771473972 (hardcover)
Classification: LCC PS8571.R776 S68 2021 | DDC jC813/.6—dc23

Edited by Katherine Dearlove | Designed by Alisa Baldwin

Manufactured in Guangdong Province, Dongguan City, China, in May 2021, by Toppan Leefung Packaging & Printing (Dongguan) Co., Ltd.
Job #BAYDC93

A   B   C   D   E   F

ONTARIO ARTS COUNCIL
CONSEIL DES ARTS DE L'ONTARIO
an Ontario government agency
un organisme du gouvernement de l'Ontario

Canada Council for the Arts   Conseil des Arts du Canada

Canada

MIX
Paper from responsible sources
FSC® C104723

Owlkids Books is a division of   bayard canada

Publisher of Chirp, Chickadee and OWL
www.owlkidsbooks.com

Sour Cakes

Written by
Karen Krossing

Illustrated by
Anna Kwan

Owlkids Books

Get up! Get up! Let's play outside!

Why out?

Today I like in.

How about a song?
We can whisper it soft.
Why soft?
Today I like
LOUD.

Then we'll yell a song

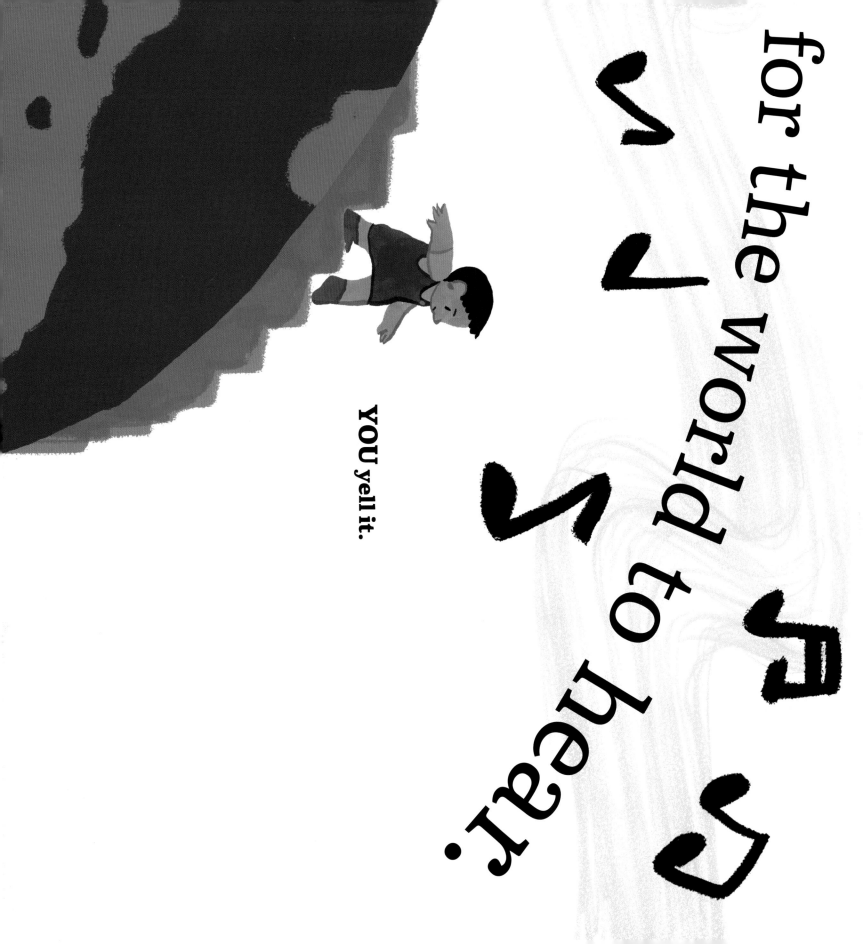

for the world to hear.

YOU yell it.

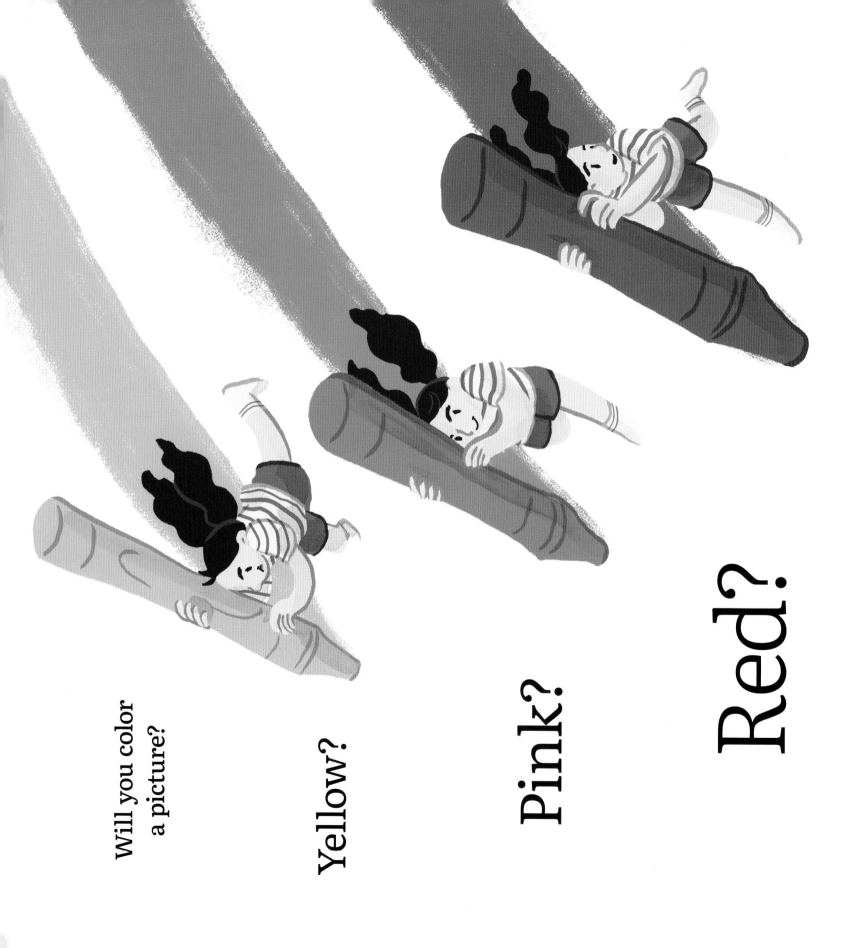

Will you color
a picture?

Yellow?

Pink?

Red?

I like gray.

Then we'll scribble with gray
till our crayons break.

YOU scribble.

You like baking treats. We'll make them taste sweet.

Why sweet?

I feel sour.

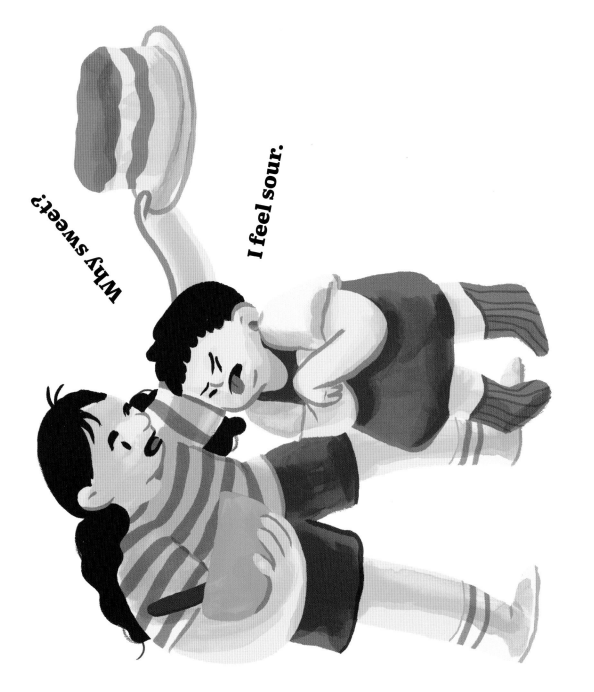

Then we'll bake sour cakes, served with—

I don't want to bake.
I don't want to color.
I don't want to **SING.**

I want the sun to **turn off.**

And the flowers to **melt away.**

I want fog
to crash down

on big monster feet.

And after that?
What do you want
after that?

And then?

I want to disappear.

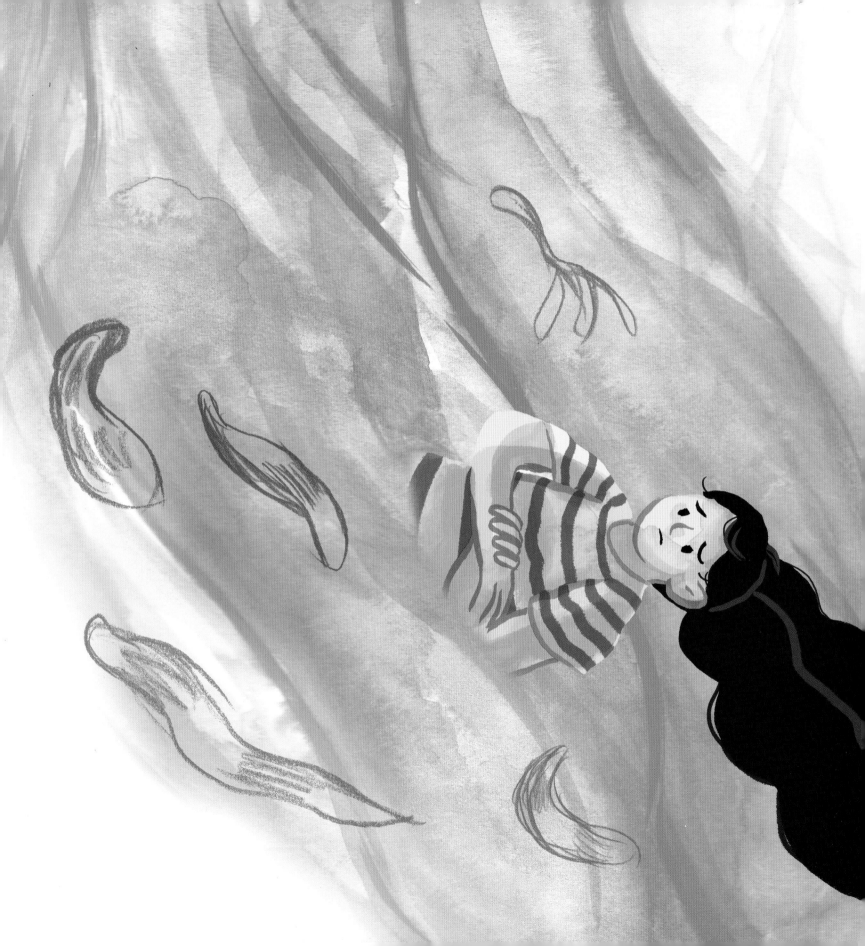

Can I disappear with you?
I could bring a song to yell.
And a picture that's gray.
And a cake that's sour—

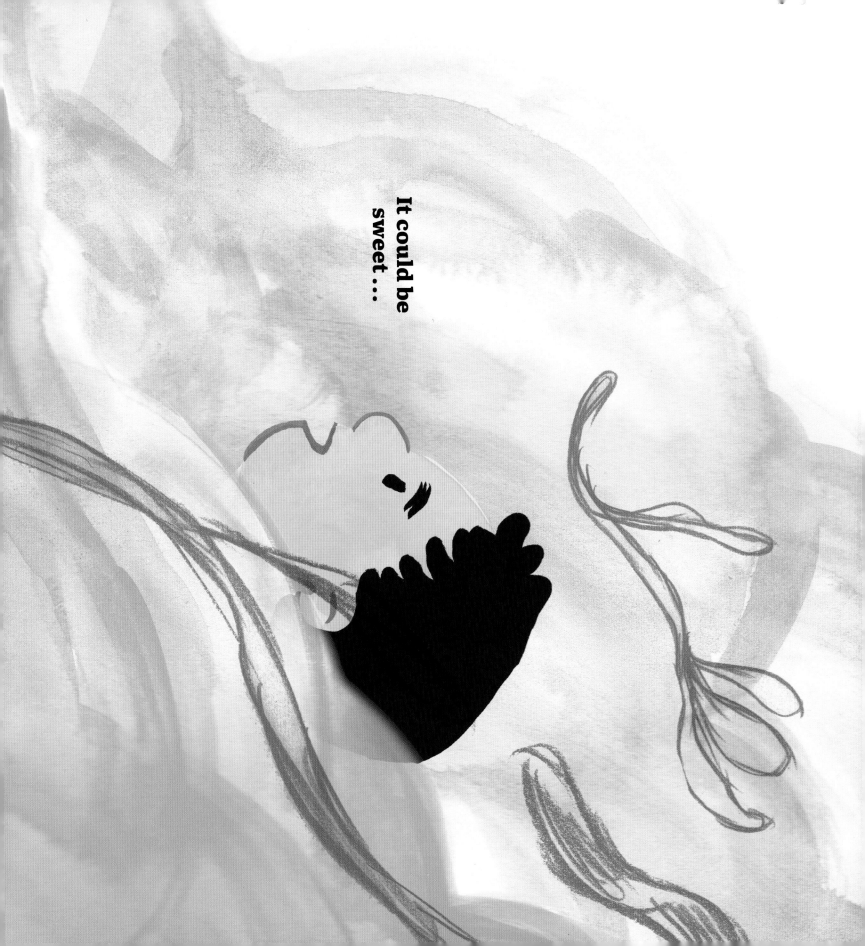

It could be
sweet . . .

Then a cake that's sweet.
We can each take a bite.

And can we dance?

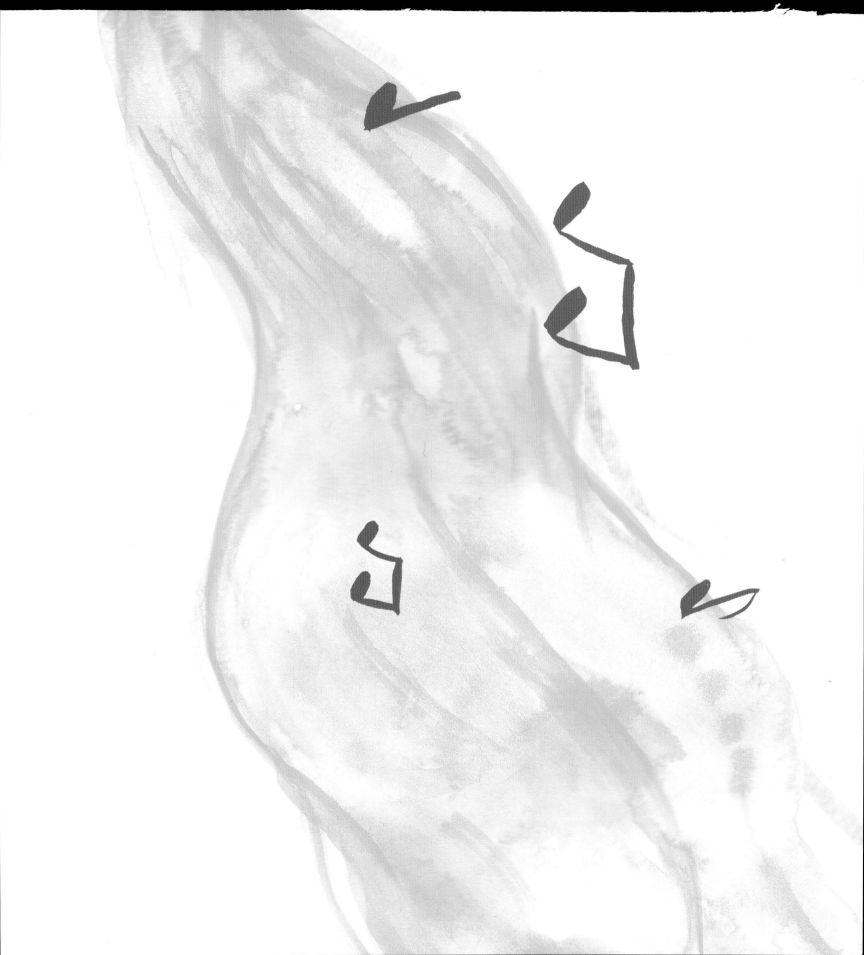

Yes, we'll dance
on big monster feet.
We'll twirl and thump …

Stomp and jump.

Till the fog
fades away?

Yes.

And then
let's play.